"I dedicate this book to the loving light that guided us all, as shone by my father, Roye Schell.

Love is love."

**PURPLE OWL PUBLISHING**
Newton, MA 02461
Copyright 2022
All rights reserved including the right of reproduction in whole or in part in any form.

# Skateboard Escape

Written and Illustrated by:

Desi Schell

# Cast of Characters

**Clockwise from left to right:**

Eldest Daughter: Zelda

Dad's life partner: Stevie (Bloke one)

Dad's illustrating partner: Robin (Bloke two)

Dad!

Middle daughter: May

Youngest daughter: Lulu

Teacup the Pup

Mom!

Featuring our Guest Star: Mitchell Marble

There once lived a family of folks,

with three little girls, one Dad and two blokes.

Mom was there too, but with dreams to pursue.

We played, we grew, we awoke!

It was summer again,

gentle smells in the breeze.

Lots of allergens in the air

causing one big sneeze!

He sprinted uncontrollably,
and jumped on the
whirring thing,
when she started up her barkin'
the chase was in full swing!

She growled with her big teeth
at this brother running in terror,
she nipped at his bare ankle
when he realized his
rolling error!

When quickly in the moment,
we saw a flash of blue,
we also saw a sneaker fly,
be glad it wasn't you!

It landed in the muddy ditch,
that skateboard of light blue.
The road had thrown a hole-y hitch
when he let out a kerchoo!

We knew that hole-y hitch
in the road,
from our "Snow Day Tumble,"
not just on snow days off
from school,
but from many kinds of bumbles!

He sneezed all over,
he coughed, he sputtered,
he may have even said, "Help!"
We discussed for a sec,
"Should we go?
What'd he say?
Don't know,
it was totally muttered!"

But not Mitchell, oh heck no!
He slowed down not at all.
His legs were in full motion
to avoid the deadly maul!

Our dachshund pup was about eight pounds,
but that didn't really matter,
because his forward motion
kept him running like Mad Hatter!

He ran right past the Gadget Shoppe,
just down and up the road.

He whooshed push-past the post office,
but he never slowed!

Propelling past the Imperial Baths,

we heard he blurred on by.

He zoomed around the corner

where he swallowed a black fly!

He shuffled past the synagogue
to be respectful of the mood.

But then he hit the gas again,
so, he didn't get chewed!

As he approached the Zen center

he reached deep down inside,

so, his feet wouldn't hit the ground

and he could float on by...

He ran and ran, not looking back,
being sure she was on his heels.
He hauled his butt through farmland,
across the golf course and atop the fields!

All while he ran
and never looking back,
May, Lu and me,
we made us a pact.

We'd gather up his sneaker
and board of light blue, too.
We laughed at the thought of him
blowing out that shoe!

We'd surely give these back to him,
and sympathetic we'd be,
but not without a laugh attack,
then run from him; we'd flee!

Even though Teacup the pup stayed back, right on our street,
he convinced himself to haul his butt, feeling her breath upon his feet!

You see he was sure that her teeth were there,
ready to bite down on his curly leg hair!
Running in terror from little Teacup!
She didn't want to eat him; she was just a wee pup!

But he'd take no chances on the idea of being eaten,
for dogs eating boys, this COULD BE the season!

He blew as he flew all throughout town. He was frazzled and sweaty when he finally slowed down.

Sheepishly, Mitchell made his way home, limping in one sneak and muddy from hi roam.

He peeked in the kitchen
to see if the dog
stood waiting to eat him...
such a little hog!

We waited for Mitchell
to come through the door,
so, we could give him his sneaker
and tell him our story
of watching from behind
as terror ran his world!
Simply dying of laughter,
we three little girls.

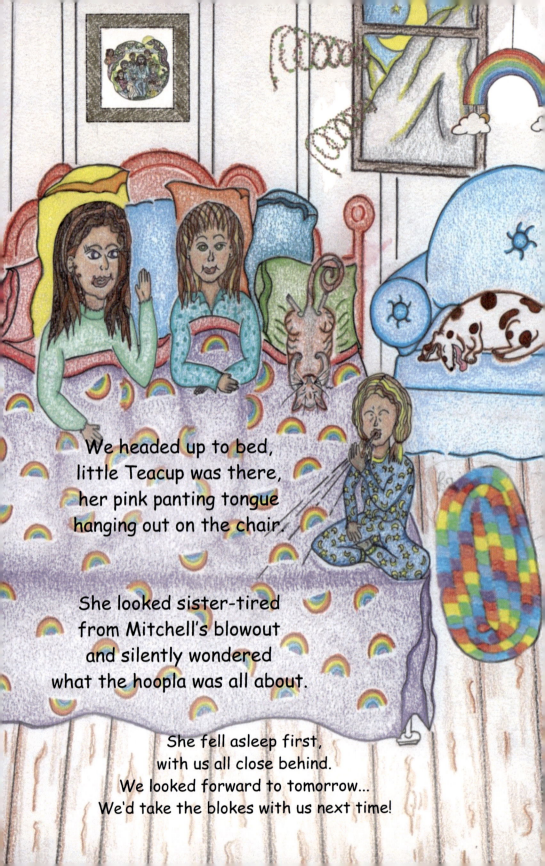

# Skateboard Escape

# Curriculum

1. During what season does the story take place?

2. What color did the girls see when Mitchell's sneaker flew?

3. Why did Mitchell run all over town? What was he feeling while running?

4. Why are the characters sneezing?

5. Which building is your favorite? Tell us why.

## Acknowledgements

A special thank you to Steven Vincent, Robin Mazey, and the studios of Mazey & Schell.

Also, thanks to Art by Macie for making the graphic version of this book great!

Desi Schell grew up in New York state, relocating to Florida in the 1980's. For the last 22 years, she taught in public schools ranging from teen parent to gifted education programs. In 2021, Desi retired from teaching and partnered with Purple Owl Publishing to bring the Home Hotel book series of children's books to the public. She enjoys sharing her dozens of stories and shaping our youth in the process. Desi and her husband live in Florida most of the time, spending some time in North Carolina each year.

Snap here for your free Skateboard Escape sticker!

Made in the USA
Middletown, DE
02 July 2022